BATMAN

THE FOG OF FEAR

WRITTEN BY
MARTIN POWELL

ILLUSTRATED BY
ERIK DOESCHER,
MIKE DECARLO AND
LEE LOUGHRIDGE

BATMAN CREATED BY
BOB KANE

Curious Fox

First published in this format in 2014 by Curious Fox,
an imprint of Capstone Global Library Limited,
7 Pilgrim Street, London, EC4V 6LB
– Registered company number: 6695582

www.curious-fox.com

CAPG33558

Art Director: Bob Lentz
Designers: Brann Garvey and Philippa Jenkins
Production Controller: Helen McCreath
Editors: Vaarunika Dharmapala, Dan Nunn and Holly Beaumont
Originated by Capstone Global Library Ltd
Printed and bound in China by Leo Paper Group

ISBN 978 1 78202 139 1
18 17 16 15 14
10 9 8 7 6 5 4 3 2 1

A CIP catalogue record for this book is available
from the British Library.

CONTENTS

CHAPTER 1

THE FOG OF FEAR

Darkness crawled across the morning sky like a giant bat from a nightmare. The residents of Gotham City stared up from the streets, or peeked out of windows, for a sign of the vanished sun. Somehow, mysteriously, it had become twilight before noon. A sudden fear of the dark gripped the entire city.

Then, a bright light sliced through the shadows. The Bat-Signal shone against the darkened clouds. It was a welcome sight for their frightened eyes.

"I never dreamed I'd have to shine the Bat-Signal in the daytime," Commissioner Gordon said. He stood on the police department rooftop. "I hope Batman sees it ... wherever he is."

The towering smokestacks of the Gotham City power plant spat a thick cloud of black fog high above the skyline. Creating its own eclipse, the darkness draped over the panicked streets. It grew like a great uncoiling snake. Before long, the bright morning spring air was as dark as midnight.

The citizens of Gotham would have been even more afraid, if they'd seen the figure atop the highest smokestack. Dressed in tatters and thin as a skeleton, the weird being shed small scraps of straw with every footstep.

He pulled a glowing jack-o'-lantern from a bag in his hand. He had already tossed several others down into the smouldering smokestack. The ragged man cackled a laugh like the sound of breaking glass.

"Trick or treat, Gotham City," the Scarecrow cried, ready to drop a pumpkin into the next chimney. "Today is Halloween – six months early!"

Schingggg!

Suddenly, a Batarang flew through the air and knocked the pumpkin out of the Scarecrow's grasp. A black-cloaked creature appeared out of nowhere, his eyes burning white-hot through the slits of his cowl.

"Not in my city," the Batman said.

Now it was the Scarecrow's turn to be afraid.

"Too late, Batman!" the Scarecrow shrieked. "You've lost already!"

Flinging his sleeves, the Scarecrow threw a clump of stinging straw into Batman's face. Like a bundle of living rags, the villain dashed around the narrow rim of the smokestack. Escape was the only thing on his evil mind.

Gripping a hooked rope, the Scarecrow prepared for his descent. Twice, he rapidly glanced behind. His eyes grew wide with surprise through the holes of his mask. Where was Batman? Among the drifting ribbons of the thick fog the Scarecrow's enemy was nowhere to be seen.

The Scarecrow quickly hurried down the long rope. An evil smile crossed his lips. Had Batman fallen to his doom? Perhaps he was finally rid of his enemy forever.

Fast as lightning, a Batarang struck the Scarecrow's glove. His fingers released the rope. The villain waved his arms helplessly and fell towards the earth below.

Batman appeared through the curtain of darkness, swinging on his Batrope. His cape flapped in the wind. In a single motion, the Caped Crusader snatched the Scarecrow from his fall.

"Don't be afraid, Scarecrow," Batman said. He gripped a small device on the rope that lowered them both gently to the ground. "I'll make sure you're safe," he said, "inside a strong prison cell."

CHAPTER 2

SINISTER SECRETS

Commissioner Gordon paced anxiously. His shoes scraped the tarred rooftop of Police Headquarters. The creeping darkness of the Scarecrow's black fog still covered the streets in shadows. Gordon was beginning to fear for his city.

"You're sure this stuff isn't poisonous, Batman?" the commissioner asked.

The Dark Knight was standing near him on the edge of the rooftop. His fluttering cape blended with the black fog.

"My lab tests confirm that this fog is not poisonous," Batman replied. "Because it's heavier than air, it will linger in Gotham City until the wind carries it out to sea. The weather will change in our favour in a few days. Until then, everyone has to get used to living in the shadows."

Commissioner Gordon frowned at the dark fog.

"That's easy for you to say, Batman," he said. "Still, I feel sorry for anyone who's scared of the dark."

Batman's eyes narrowed. "That's just it," he said. "The Scarecrow works through fear. Even after I captured him at the power plant, he seemed strangely sure of himself. It's as if he still has some fearful secret that I haven't worked out yet."

"Gotham City is safe because of you," said Commissioner Gordon. "At least the threat of the Scarecrow is over, and he is safely locked up."

The Dark Knight shook his head thoughtfully. "It's not over yet, old friend," he said quietly.

• • •

It was always dark in the Batcave, secretly located beneath Wayne Manor. Later that afternoon, inside the hidden cavern, Batman removed his cape and cowl, revealing the face of billionaire Bruce Wayne. Wayne peered into a high-powered microscope. He fought a yawn, rubbed his tired eyes, and got back to work.

Behind Bruce rose a tall, dark set of stairs. Alfred the butler was coming down the stairs into the underground laboratory. "Miss Kyle called, Master Bruce. She's waiting to meet you for lunch at the restaurant," said Alfred.

Bruce prepared a thin orange-coloured slice upon a glass slide. He added a drop of a glowing chemical.

"Call her back with my apologies, Alfred," he said. "It's going to be as dark as night in Gotham City for the next few days. Commissioner Gordon's policemen are working 24-hour shifts. Batman can do no less."

Alfred peeked over Bruce's shoulder. He stared at a strange orange vegetable sitting on the table.

"Isn't it a bit early for carving pumpkins, sir?" Alfred asked.

Bruce smiled. "This belonged to the Scarecrow," he explained. "He filled these pumpkins with a secret chemical before tossing them into the power plant smokestacks. The result was the black fog that is still plaguing the city."

"Well, sir," offered Alfred, "I'll admit this fog is troubling. However, it's hardly the same kind of trick the Scarecrow has used against you in the past."

Bruce rose quickly, grabbing his black cowl and cloak. "Exactly," he said. Bruce filled the compartments of his Utility Belt. "There's more to this black fog than meets the eye. And, one way or the other, the Scarecrow is going to tell me its secret."

Arkham Asylum was like a madhouse from another world. Locked within its electrified iron gates lived the deadliest criminals ever known. Even in the daylight, the building looked like a bad dream. The black fog added even more to its eeriness.

The headlights of the Batmobile sliced through the inky clouds of fog. The front guards saluted as Batman stepped out of the vehicle. He passed into the dreadful place without a word. Caged doors opened before him with a motorized hum. The Dark Knight knew his way through the twisted corridors all too well.

"If I'd known you were coming, I'd have baked a Bat-cake!" a voice giggled from behind a cell door.

Batman stopped and glared at the white face pressed against the bars.

"Joker," he said through gritted teeth.

The Joker's blood-red lips continued to curl upwards towards his yellow eyes. Batman's face remained like stone, unsmiling. On reflex, his gloved fists tightly clenched.

"Hey, Bats! When are you going to bring back the sunshine?" the Joker said. A chuckle hissed between his teeth.

"What's the matter, Joker?" asked Batman. "Afraid of the dark?"

"You've got to be joking, Bat-brain!" the killer clown gleefully cried. "I just want to know when you're going to ruin the Scarecrow's party! He's been raving about his 'crime of the century' for hours. Such a bore. Frankly, just between us boys, I think he's nutty as a filbert!"

Batman whirled from the cell. He had to focus on the problem at hand. The mystery of the Scarecrow was waiting to be solved.

Jonathan Crane had once been a brilliant professor of psychology. He specialized in the study of fear. That was before his mind snapped and he turned to crime. As the Scarecrow, Crane had always been defeated by Batman, no matter how ingenious his crimes. This time Crane was certain things were going to be different.

Crane looked almost harmless without his fearsome costume. Tall and thin with an evil smirk on his face, he sat in his cell quietly reading. Batman studied him silently for several minutes.

"I'm only going to ask you this once, Crane," the Dark Knight warned. "What's the secret of the black fog?"

Crane continued reading, as if he'd heard nothing. Then he smiled smugly.

"You'll know soon enough, Batman," the evil genius replied. "Now, if you'll excuse me, I'm trying to broaden my mind."

Batman's brain worked at top speed. He read the titles of the volumes on Crane's crammed bookshelves. Many of the books were old. Some were ancient. Most of them seemed to be about the so-called "four elements": fire, water, earth and air. Hundreds of years ago, men called alchemists believed that the world was made of just these four ingredients.

Could Crane's formula be related to the four elements? wondered Batman.

Immediately, the Dark Knight had the answer.

SCARECROW
CRANE

'Earth' would equal the jack-o'-lanterns. 'Fire' was added from the power plant smokestacks. 'Air' joined the mix, forming the black fog. One element was missing: a single ingredient that would turn the black fog deadly.

"Water!" Batman exclaimed.

RUMMMMMMMMMMMBLE! Batman's blood ran cold. His sharp ears caught the rumble of an approaching thunderstorm.

From out of Crane's thin lips came the Scarecrow's awful laugh.

CHAPTER 3

CLOUDED BY FEAR

Commissioner Gordon leaned against his office desk to steady himself. The news Batman had brought was shocking. Gordon knew that the Dark Knight was almost never wrong.

"If what you're saying is true, Batman," he said, "then all of Gotham is about to be scared to death!"

"There's no doubt about it," Batman assured him. "When I visited Scarecrow's cell, I solved the mystery of his plan. I detected the poison in his formula."

"Once this black fog is mixed with water," Batman continued, "all who breathe it will experience their most dreadful fears. Unless we act quickly, the city is doomed to be trapped forever inside their worst nightmares."

Gordon went to the window and glanced outside. It was just past three o'clock in the afternoon, yet the sky was still dark as midnight. The Bat-Signal was still burning against the black clouds, just as the Commissioner had ordered. Its presence gave looters and other criminals second thoughts. The Bat-Signal also gave hope to Gotham City's honest citizens.

BRROOOOMMMM!! The approaching thunderstorm growled in the distance. Jagged shards of lightning flashed on the horizon.

"This coming storm will drench the city in terror," Gordon said. He thumped his fist hard against the sill. "Is there anything that can be done?"

Batman nodded. "We can clean the air of the black fog before the rain begins," he said. He sounded confident, in spite of the odds against him.

Commissioner Gordon spun on his heels. He greatly respected his friend, but this idea sounded impossible.

"But how, Batman?" he asked. "You said that there won't be enough wind in Gotham for days. How can we possibly speed up Mother Nature?"

The Caped Crusader moved to the window and opened it. He fired a grapple and rope to a neighbouring building.

"With our courage and our wits," Batman remarked.

FWOOOSHHHHHH!! He swung away, disappearing into the murky air.

Batman swooped high above the streets of Gotham City. People down below saw the shadow of a huge bat flying through the strange fog. None of them knew it was really the Caped Crusader.

Batman used his rope and grappling device to swing from building to building. His goal was a tall, white skyscraper near the edge of the city. Inside the building was a high-tech laboratory owned by one of the world's greatest scientists, Dr Kirk Langstrom. Batman hoped that Langstrom's science would be strong enough to defeat the Scarecrow's evil formula.

As the Dark Knight swooped through the fog, tiny water droplets collected on his armoured suit. The mist pressed cold and damp against his cowl.

Without warning, Batman's rope changed shape. Instead of a thin silken cord, he was holding on to a deadly boa constrictor.

"What –?" yelled Batman. He released his grip on the snake and began to fall.

Batman shot a grappling hook towards another nearby building. ZING! Just in time, the new rope pulled him upwards. He barely missed hitting a statue coming out from the side of an office building.

That was close, thought Batman. *But what is going on?*

Again, his rope transformed. This time it turned into a super sticky web. A monstrous spider snapped its drooling jaws. Its giant head thrust towards the startled hero.

"You can't be real," said Batman, shaking his head. He shot out his feet and swung quickly around his rope, building up speed. Then he aimed his boots at the fearsome mouth of the spider. Instead of feeling the impact, Batman's feet met nothing but air.

It's an illusion, he thought. *It must be the mist. There's just enough water in the air to combine with the black smoke and make me see things.*

Batman frowned. *If this is how the Scarecrow's fog can affect the brain with just a little water, then the rainstorm will create a total panic.*

Batman increased his speed and swung back towards the white skyscraper. Things were worse than he imagined.

CHAPTER 4

THE LIVING NIGHTMARE

"I knew I could count on you, Kirk," Batman said. He shook the scientist's hand.

Kirk Langstrom stood in his white lab coat, a deep contrast to Batman's black and grey Batsuit. Still, the two men shared at least two traits. Both were brilliant. Both wanted to save their city.

"You cured me, Batman. I owe you everything," Langstrom replied. "When I experimented with the bat-serum, I turned into the monster, Man-Bat."

"You were the only one who helped me," said Langstrom. "I'll never forget that."

The Dark Knight remembered those frightening nights when his friend had changed into a powerful creature. Although not truly evil, the Man-Bat was wild and uncontrollable. Those memories were like a nightmare to both men.

"This is Gotham's only hope," Batman stated. "You are the world's greatest living expert on bats."

"Takes one to know one, I guess," Langstrom said. He smiled, almost sadly, as he unveiled his experimental machine.

The device on Langstrom's laboratory workbench looked like something from a science fiction film. It was made of blinking lights and coiling wires.

Batman noticed that Langstrom himself stared at the machine with dread. As much as the scientist wanted to help, he was still hiding something.

"I haven't tested it yet," Langstrom said quietly. "But if it works, the machine should send out a high-pitched sound. The sound can only be heard by the sensitive ears of bats. Millions of them will be awakened by this sound, flying to wherever it leads them."

Batman was impressed. The machine was exactly what he needed.

"That's all I need to know," he said, reaching for the device.

The Dark Knight slowly flipped a small switch.

The machine glowed, then started to hum. Although Batman could feel only a slight vibration in the air, Langstrom's ears immediately began to ache.

Within minutes, hundreds of bats swooped and fluttered against the window of the lab.

"It works!" cried Langstrom.

Batman turned off the machine, well satisfied.

"It's perfect, Kirk," he said. "I have just enough time to get this machine back to the Batcave before the thunderstorm starts."

There was an eerie silence in the room. Langstrom had retreated into a far corner, away from the harsh light in the lab.

Batman was alarmed by the sounds of the scientist's heavy breaths. He took a step towards his friend.

"Kirk? Are you all right?" he asked.

No answer came from the dark corner. Then Batman heard the sounds of more rapid breathing. He heard a slow ripping of cloth. Then he saw a sudden spreading of monstrous wings.

The Man-Bat had returned. Langstrom had been transformed by the effect of his sound machine!

The Dark Knight braced himself as he saw the burning red eyes glare at him. The creature leaped forward. Batman was driven back by the muscular weight of the monster. He crashed backwards through tables of shattering glass.

There was no more expert fighter in the world than the Batman. But for a moment, even his fists were useless against the strength and speed of the Man-Bat.

The beast's claws gripped Batman's throat with a blur of motion. Sharp teeth gleamed behind the gruesome growl. Batman's brain was spinning, close to blacking out. His gloved fingers groped for his Utility Belt, his only chance.

FLASH! A bright flare shone in Batman's hand. The Man-Bat howled in rage. It flung itself through the window.

The Dark Knight caught his breath. He watched the Man-Bat escape into the gloomy sky, carried by its giant wings.

"You feared this would happen, didn't you?" Batman said to himself. "Kirk, why didn't you tell me?"

BATMAN VS MAN-BAT

Less than an hour later, the Batplane screamed out of the Gotham sky. The storm was almost upon the city. There wasn't a moment to lose.

Kirk Langstrom's amazing invention was wired into an amplifier within the plane's cockpit. All Batman needed to do was press the switch … and hope.

The sound was much too high for the Dark Knight's human ears. Several minutes passed before he knew for sure that it was operating. Then, suddenly, there they were.

"Bats!"

The bats obeyed the sound machine, following close behind the Batplane. They came in an endless stream, thousands and thousands of them. Countless tiny wings flapped through the air. Soon, the black fog softened to grey. The sky was alive with the swarm of fluttering wings.

The Batplane streaked through the clouds. It rocketed above rooftops and sliced between buildings. The bats followed, sweeping away the fog with every beat of their leathery wings. In a few minutes the Scarecrow's black fog was no more.

Batman turned off the sound machine. The swarm of bats cleared the skies and returned to their hidden lairs. The Dark Knight was about to breathe a sigh of relief when another threat struck from the sky.

WHAM! Something hard collided against the hull of the Batplane. Batman saw the jagged wings and glowing eyes of his attacker.

The Man-Bat had also answered the call of the machine. In a mindless rage, the Man-Bat struck the Batplane. Batman fought hard to regain control. He had to take this battle down to the ground, out of the Man-Bat's element. His sharp eyes found a safe place to land – an old cemetery outside the city.

The Batplane glided down among the twisted trees and tombstones. It came to a stop just as the rain started to fall.

Leaping from the cockpit, Batman peered skywards. The rain poured down, making it hard to see.

The Man-Bat was fast and strong. The Dark Knight knew he would only get one chance to defeat the beast.

A furious flash of lightning revealed the Man-Bat, swooping out of the sky like a prehistoric monster. Batman dropped and rolled away as the creature's deadly talons grabbed only mud. Again the flying fiend shot towards Batman like a demon, but its claws found only open air. A spinning kick to the creature's chest finally brought the Man-Bat to earth.

The monster rose up from the mud, towering above Batman. Pain and hatred grew in the Man-Bat's mind. It let out a terrible snarl. Batman's right hand went to his Utility Belt, retrieving an item, which he hid behind his glove.

"Kirk!" Batman said. He tried to calm the beast. "I want to help you. Kirk, don't you know me?"

The Man-Bat's wild eyes softened a moment. The creature tilted its head in confusion. Batman approached the creature slowly. Deadly as Man-Bat might be, Batman had to get close enough to touch.

A sudden clap of thunder startled the beast. ROOAAARRR!!

Its clawed wings wrapped tightly around Batman's throat. Nothing could break the monstrous grip. It was too strong. But the Dark Knight's right hand was free, and that was all he needed. He made a quick move, pressing a sharp object against the creature's hide.

The Man-Bat released its stranglehold in a snap. It appeared to grow dizzy and staggered. Finally, it dropped to its shaggy knees.

The Batman returned the object to his Utility Belt. It was a needle that had contained the antidote to the Man-Bat formula.

Before Batman's eyes, the giant beast seemed to shrink. Its fur slowly melted away. The huge wings grew smaller and disappeared. In a few moments, scientist Kirk Langstrom crouched in the creature's place. Batman carefully helped his friend stand.

"Batman?" Langstrom asked. "What have I done?" He remembered nothing from the past few hours.

Batman placed a grateful hand on Langstrom's shoulder. "You saved the city, Kirk," he said softly. "The black fog is gone, blown away by the wings of bats. Your machine worked just as you said. You're a hero."

The storm was over. The rain had ended, and the Scarecrow's evil nightmares vanished with the coming sunshine.

"I had a terrible dream about Man-Bat," said Langstrom, confused. "I was afraid he had come back. Afraid he'd try to hurt you."

Batman smiled. "Nothing to be afraid of now," he said.

It was going to be a beautiful day in Gotham City.

Scarecrow, The

REAL NAME: Professor Jonathan Crane

OCCUPATION: Professional criminal

BASE: Gotham City

HEIGHT:
6 feet

WEIGHT:
10 stone

EYES:
Blue

HAIR:
Brown

Jonathan Crane's obsession with fear took hold at an early age. Terrorized by bullies, Crane sought to free himself of his own worst fears. As he researched the subject of dread, Crane developed a strong understanding of fear. Using this knowledge, Crane overcame his tormentors by using their worst fears against them. This victory led to his transformation into the creepy super-villain, the Scarecrow.

G.C.P.D. GOTHAM CITY POLICE DEPARTMENT

- *Crane became a professor at Gotham University to further his terrifying research. But when his colleagues took notice of his twisted experiments, they had him fired. To get revenge, Crane became the Scarecrow to try to frighten his enemies to death.*

- *Crane doesn't use conventional weaponry. Instead, he invented a fear toxin that causes his victims to hallucinate, bringing their worst fears and phobias to life. The gas makes the weak and gangly Crane look like a fearsome predator in the eyes of his prey.*

- *Even though he preys on the fears of others, the Scarecrow has a fear of his own – bats! Crane has been chiropteraphobic, or afraid of bats, since his first encounter with the Dark Knight.*

- *Crane's mastery of fear has come in handy. While locked up in Arkham Asylum, Crane escaped from his cell by scaring two guards into releasing him!*

CONFIDENTIAL

Other CURIOUS FOX titles you might be interested in...

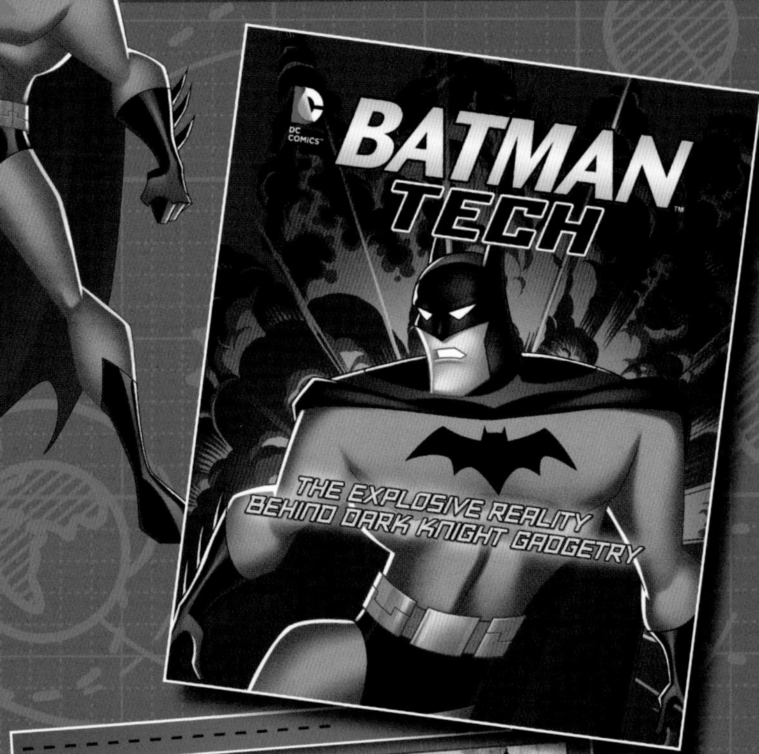

BODY ARMOUR

To fight crime, Batman puts himself in the line of fire. The Batsuit is the only thing that stands between him and all kinds of lethal impacts. To protect him, it includes body armour – a technology that has come a long way over the centuries.

The history of body armour spans thousands of years. Ancient tribes used animal hides and woven plant material for protection from cuts and scrapes. The ancient Romans covered their chests with metal breastplates. Full-body metal armour came into its glory by the 1400s. Medieval knights covered themselves from head to toe in metal plates to protect against sword thrusts or arrows.

Once cannons and guns were developed, traditional armour fell by the wayside. To protect from these kinds of impacts, metal armour would be too heavy to wear.

Medieval knights protected themselves with heavy metal armour.

Soldiers put on armoured bomb suits before disabling explosive devices.

But as weapons have changed, body armour has evolved too. Today soldiers and police protect themselves with either hard or soft body armour. Hard body armour is similar to the metal armour of the Middle Ages. It protects well, but is heavy and cumbersome.

Soft body armour is woven out of advanced materials sewn into vests and other clothing. It is much more comfortable than wearing heavy metal plates. The most famous material used in soft body armour is Kevlar.

62 63

DC COMICS™
SUPER HEROES

Curious Fox

SUPERMAN™

THE DEADLY DOUBLE

LITTLE GREEN MEN

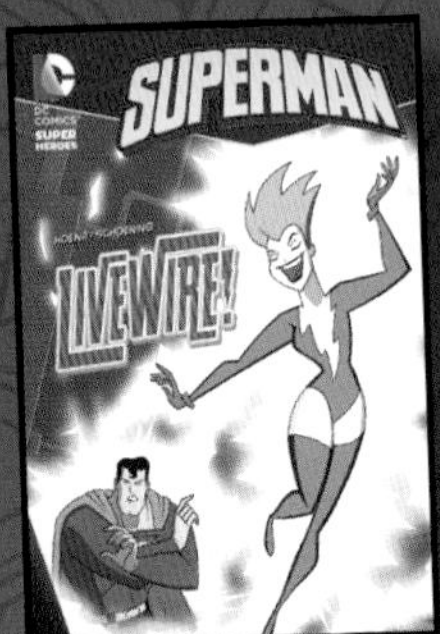

LIVEWIRE!

PRANKSTER OF PRIME TIME

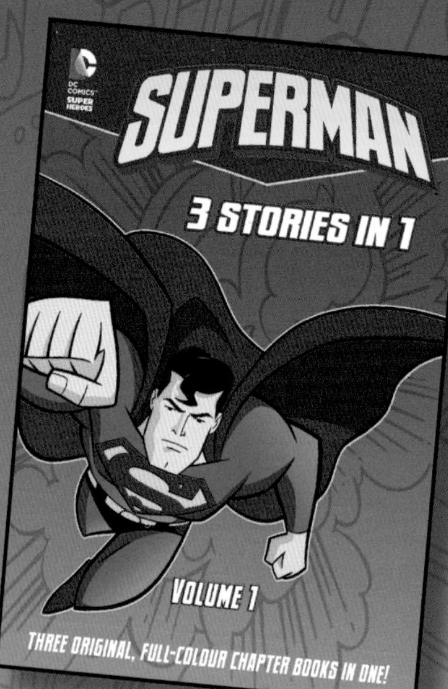

3 STORIES IN 1

METEOR OF DOOM

DC
COMICS™
SUPER
HEROES

BATMAN™

SCARECROW, DOCTOR OF FEAR

THE FOG OF FEAR

MAD HATTER'S MOVIE MADNESS

THE REVENGE OF CLAYFACE

3 STORIES IN 1

ROBIN'S FIRST FLIGHT